TESS

by H.J. Hutchins

illustrated
by Ruth Ohi

Annick Press Ltd.
Toronto • New York

Annick Press Ltd.

Annick Press gratefully acknowledges the support of
the Canada Council and the Ontario Arts Council.

Canadian Cataloguing in Publication Data

Hutchins, H. J. (Hazel J.)
   Tess

ISBN 1-55037-395-1 (bound) ISBN 1-55037-394-3 (pbk.)

I. Ohi, Ruth.   II. Title.

PS8565.U826T4 1995   jC813'.54   C95-930659-5
PZ7.H87Te 1995

The art in this book was rendered in watercolours.
The text was typeset in Century Oldstyle.

Distributed in Canada by:
Firefly Books Ltd.
250 Sparks Avenue
Willowdale, ON
M2H 2S4

Published in the U.S.A. by Annick Press (U.S.) Ltd.
Distributed in the U.S.A. by:
Firefly Books (U.S.) Inc.
P.O. Box 1338
Ellicott Station
Buffalo, NY 14205

Printed and bound in Canada by
Metropole Litho.

To Margaret Gilkes
my wonderful Aunt Mag
who has lived many good stories
and written many good stories
and been kind enough to let me borrow this one.
—H.H.—

For AAUU.
—R.O.—

When Tess was a young girl she lived in a
tiny shack with her mother and father and two
older brothers and the prairie all around.

Tess loved the prairie. She rode Chinook, her
fiery pony, full clip across the grasslands. She
explored along the coulees. At night she lay
outside to listen to the coyotes howl.

Her mother and father did not love the prairie. They had come from warmer places and gentler society. They found it hard to live in a land that was new to them. Tess saw it in their faces. She saw it that spring day when there were only a few shovelfuls of coal left in the shed and no money to buy more until the fall harvest.

"And we have to cook," said her mother.

"And there are still days when we'll need heat in the house," said her father.

They decided to use a fuel they had seen others burn in the country from which they had come. It had a pleasant, melodic name that sounded like "malongo." Tess and her brother Charlie were sent out to gather it.

"Cow patties!" said Charlie in disgust. "We have to gather cow patties!"

"Not cow patties," said Tess. "Malongo. People do it all the time in other places."

"They don't do it here," said Charlie.

That was true. And, although their parents had assured them this was a perfectly proper activity, Tess and Charlie also understood that it would be best if no one else knew. If a neighbour's wagon or automobile drove into the yard while they were out gathering, the sacks were to be left in the fields. The last of the coal was saved for company.

The first batch of malongo was an interesting experiment. If the patty was too fresh it burned with a thick smoke and a frightful smell. If it was too old it crumbled and was no use at all. Soon, however, Tess and Charlie learned to recognize patties of exactly the right age and texture. By summer, in fact, the quest for perfect malongo had become, not a chore, but a challenge between them—a great and glorious treasure hunt.

They raced across the pasture land, they slid down the coulee sides, they searched even the fringes of the neighbours' land—as long as they could do so out of sight of the neighbours' houses—for the biggest and best malongo to fill their sacks.

One day at the end of summer, however, when Tess was first to fill her sack and come laughing around the barn into the yard, she ran smack into a neighbour.

Mr. Wright was a big man—big and haughty and unforgiving. He lived alone on the farm beyond the coulee. There was no wagon in the yard, so he and his young dog must have walked over.

Mr. Wright looked down at Tess. He looked down at the sack piled high with malongo. It took him a moment to understand, but when he did his lip curled in a sneer.

"Cow manure," he said, scornful. "That's what it is makes your house smell so odd. You burn cow manure."

He threw his head back and sniffed loudly.

"Ha!" he said, and went on his way.

Tess felt ashamed and angry, and, worst of all, she felt she'd let her family down. Slowly she put the sack under the eaves of the coal shed. Quietly she went into the house. She didn't tell anyone about Mr. Wright. She tried to bury it all away inside her.

When harvest was over that fall there was still not much money, but there was money for coal. That was good, because winters were cold when Tess was a girl. Frost formed on the boards inside the shack, the blankets froze against the walls, the water froze in the wash basin. Tess and Charlie rode their horses bareback to try and keep warm on their way to school. When they got there, the ink was frozen in the inkwells and their brown-bread-and-lard sandwiches were frozen in the pails in which they carried them.

But sledding was a good way to stay warm. And skating on the slough was a good way. And in the evenings around the stove—where the coal burned hot and red—Tess's mother read exciting stories of far-off countries and noble heroes, and poetry that surged like a swiftly galloping pony.

One morning, when Tess was going to get her own noble pony from the barn, she saw something that did not seem right. The coyotes were about.

She saw their shadowy forms rise to the lip of the coulee, look over, and slide out of sight again.

And then she saw, halfway between her farm and the Wright place, Mr. Wright's dog and a single coyote, playing out on the snows. They were playing and weaving and doing a kind of little dance on the white flatness, except the dance led every moment closer and closer to the coulee.

Quickly Tess ran to the barn. She knew the coyote wasn't playing. It was leading the young dog into a trap.

Her fingers fumbled in their haste as she slipped a rope through Chinook's halter. She whistled for their own lumbering hunting dog, Sampson, and grabbed a rope from the corral post. She slid her hand into Chinook's thick mane and swung aboard.

"Hurry, Chinook. Hurry."

Across the snowy pasture to the lip of the coulee they raced. There below was the young dog and the coyotes and—oh!—already they had turned on him. They had come in as a pack, circling and rushing in, circling and rushing in.

"Yaaaaaaaaaaaah!" cried Tess.

Like a winter storm they flew down the snowy slope—the fearless Chinook and the great howling Sampson and Tess yelling and flailing with the rope.

The coyotes reeled and fled. Sampson gave chase, but Tess knew he was too wise to follow them far. She bent over Mr. Wright's dog. One haunch was torn and his fur was wet and matted from wounds she could not see. His whole body was trembling, shaking.

As carefully as she could, Tess gathered him in her arms and struggled up out of the coulee.
CRACK!

—A rifle shot split the air. Across the fields, the figure of Mr. Wright was hurrying, his rifle pointed high. As he drew closer and recognized them, Tess could hear him scolding.

"I tell him, the young fool, stay away from coyotes. I tell him."

But when he saw how badly the dog was hurt, he grew silent. He took off his coat and wrapped the dog in it as he lifted the now-limp body out of Tess's aching arms.

Not in time, thought Tess despairingly as she watched them go, I was not in time.

On the prairies, when spring comes it comes in a rush. The snow melts and suddenly there is water everywhere. Wild geese come calling up the wind and crocuses break through the brown grasses, and soon, as the ground begins to dry on the southern coulee slopes, dry malongo appears.

Tess hoped that this year they would not have to go gathering. However, her parents counted the money in the tobacco tin, and the next day Charlie and Tess were sent out on their quest.

The world was full of life that day and Tess
could not be unhappy for long. She watched the
newly-returned burrowing owls. She found the
carefully-hidden magic of a duck's nest.
Even after Charlie had filled his sack and gone
back to the house, Tess kept wandering. It all

seemed to speak to her—that great sweep of prairie and the sky so wide, so wide that it made her feel wonderfully small and wonderfully grand all at once. She didn't care if they were poor and had to gather malongo. How could you be poor with the whole prairie at your feet?

So great was her feeling that when she finally did turn for home, and saw Mr. Wright's wagon in their yard, she didn't stop to worry about what was in her sack. She came swinging through the yard, bold as brass, and laid it beneath the eaves of the shed...and there she stopped. Four sacks of malongo. There should only be two—hers and Charlie's. Where had the other two come from? For a long moment she just stood there, puzzled.

Then she heard a slight noise behind her. She turned. Mr. Wright was standing at the corner of the shed. He looked every bit as big and haughty and unforgiving as he always did. He was, however, doing something very strange with his eye. He seemed to be trying to wink.

An incredible thought came to Tess. Had old Mr. Wright—serious, haughty, unforgiving Mr. Wright—been gathering sacks of malongo? Was he making fun of her? Or was he, after many grumpy years of living alone, going quietly mad?

A moment later the answer came trotting around the corner and sat companionably at the old man's feet. It was Mr. Wright's dog—a little older, and, she hoped, a little wiser—but very much alive.

"He made it," said Tess. "I did get there in time!"

The old man reached down and gave the dog an affectionate rub.

Tess didn't know what else to say. Neither, apparently, did Mr. Wright. Finally he tilted his head back and sniffed loudly.

"Ha," he said.

He turned, climbed up into the wagon, and drove away.

When Tess was a young girl she lived in a tiny shack with her mother and father and two older brothers and the prairie all around.

And a neighbour who sometimes helped her gather cow manure for their summer fuel.